MOTHER and FATHER

TULIP

TUCKER and STITCH

STITCH

To Al and our children,
Mac, Erin, Sam

With grateful appreciation to Sue Hill
for her help in telling the story.

Tucker's Four-Carrot School Day • Copyright © 2005 by Susan Winget • Manufactured in China by South China Printing Company Ltd. • All rights reserved. • www.harperchildrens.com • Library of Congress Cataloging-in-Publication Data • Winget, Susan. • Tucker's four-carrot school day / by Susan Winget.—1st ed. • p. cm. • Summary: The start of Tucker the rabbit's first day of kindergarten is rocky, but making new friends helps change his attitude toward school. • ISBN 0-06-054642-5 — ISBN 0-06-054643-3 (lib. bdg.) • [1. First day of school--Fiction. 2. Kindergarten--Fiction. 3. Schools--Fiction. 4. Friendship--Fiction. 5. Rabbits--Fiction.] I. Title. • PZ7.W7284Tu • 2005 • [E]--dc22 • 2004004178 • Design by Stephanie Bart-Horvath • 1 2 3 4 5 6 7 8 9 10 • ❖ • First Edition

Tucker's Four-Carrot School Day

Susan Winget

HarperCollins Publishers

"Where's Tucker?" asked Tucker's father.

Tucker peeked out of hiding.
"I don't want to go to school,"
he said.

"Hey, I remember the
first time I went to
school," Father said.
"I was scared!"
"You were?"
"Yes, but I did it and
you can, too!"

"Can Stitch come with me?" asked Tucker.
"You bet," said Tucker's father.

Tucker got ready.

Mother and Tulip
packed a surprise
in Tucker's backpack.

Then they walked down the street to school.

"Maybe I better not go in," said Tucker.
"Won't you and Tulip miss me?"

"Of course we'll miss you, Tucker. But I just know you'll be great at school." Tucker's mother gave him a big hug.

Tucker felt better, but Tulip looked sad. "Here, Tulip," Tucker said. "You can play with Stitch today."

"Come on in, Tucker," said the teacher.
"Um, Miss Blossom?" Tucker began.
"I need to go home. I help take care of my sister."

"I bet you're a good helper," said Miss Blossom.
"Can you help me put out the paints?"
"Sure!" said Tucker. "I love to paint!"

But Tucker tripped and paint spilled everywhere.
What a big mess! Tucker felt like all the other
children were looking at him.

"I . . . I'm sorry,"
he whispered.

"It's all right, Tucker," said Miss Blossom.
"Making a mess is part of the fun!"

Before long everyone was painting.
Tucker made his truck bright blue.

After painting, it was music time.

All the children sang and played. Tucker was having fun!

La-La-La!

When the song ended,
Tucker just kept going.

The other children
laughed.

"Oops," said Tucker.

"Let's all sing one more song with Tucker!" said Miss Blossom.

At nap time, Tucker went to get Stitch from his backpack. But Stitch wasn't there. . . . Stitch was with Tulip.

I miss Stitch, Tucker thought. I miss home.

Then he saw something in the bottom of his backpack. He reached in and pulled out a picture. There was his whole family, even Stitch!

Suddenly Tucker didn't feel quite so homesick.

At playtime, Jonathan and Jared
were building a tall tower.

"I'm good at blocks,"
said Tucker.
He added one to
the top.

Millie went next. Her
block made the tower
tumble to the ground!
"Sorry!" said Millie.
"That's okay," said
Tucker. "Knocking it
down is the best part."

Soon it was snack time. Miss Blossom gave
everyone an apple and an oatmeal-raisin cookie.

"I don't want an apple," Millie said.

"I don't like raisins in cookies," said Tucker. "Let's trade!"

Before Tucker knew it, the school day was over.
His mother was waiting to walk him home.
Tucker waved good-bye to his new friends.

"Bye, Tucker!" said Millie.
"Bye, Millie!" said Tucker.

"Tell us about your day," Father said.

La La La

"Well . . . first I spilled paint. Then I sang loud when everybody else was quiet. La La La

"But then everybody sang with me! And Millie gave me her apple and I gave her my cookie—and I brought home a picture."

Mother put Tucker's picture on the refrigerator.
Father said, "Tucker, it sounds like you've had a
four-carrot day!

"You painted a picture, you helped the teacher, and
you made some new friends."
Mother and Father said, "We're so proud of you."

"Yay, Tucker," said Tulip.
Tucker smiled and said,
"I did it and you can, too!"

MISS BLOSSOM

TUCKER'S SCHOOL

Tucker